DOLAN, Penny

Roly-poly rice ball

First published in 2003 by
Franklin Watts
338 Euston Road
London
NW1 3BH

Franklin Watts Australia
Hachette Children's Books
Level 17/207 Kent Street
Sydney
NSW 2000

A CIP catalogue record for this book is available
from the British Library.

ISBN (10) 0 7496 5333 7 (pbk)
ISBN (13) 978-0-7496-5333-0 (pbk)

Series Editor: Jackie Hamley
Series Advisor: Dr Barrie Wade
Series Designer: Peter Scoulding

Printed in China

Roly-poly Rice Ball

by Penny Dolan and Diana Mayo

FRANKLIN WATTS

LONDON • SYDNEY

All morning, Li swept the path
clean for the rich people to walk on.

Then Li sat under the cherry tree
and unfolded his lunch-cloth.
There lay three rice balls, as white
and round as three tiny moons.

Li sighed. His rice box at home was now empty. What would he eat for supper tonight?

Suddenly, Li heard tiny voices singing: "Roly-poly rice ball, roly-poly rice ball, roly-poly rice ball, roll right IN!"

One rice ball jumped off Li's cloth,
and rolled down a hole under the
cherry tree.

The voices sang
again: "Roly-poly rice
ball, roll right IN!" Li saw
his second rice ball roly-poly
down the hole.
Then the third!

Li bent down and heard
laughing and singing
down the tunnel.

"I hope you enjoy my rice balls,
whoever you are!" he cried.

"Roly-poly rice ball, roll right IN!" came the voices. And this time Li went roly-poly down the tunnel!

Li rolled into a tiny underground
palace. Lots of mice, dressed in fine
robes, nibbled away at Li's rice balls.

The Mouse Emperor sat high on his
throne. He smiled at Li. Li smiled
back, though he felt very hungry.

The Emperor clapped his paws.
The old mice played music on tiny
instruments. It was as sweet as the
birds singing in the cherry tree.

The Emperor smiled. So did Li,
though he was still very hungry.

Then the young mice danced
together, waving their painted
fans. They were as pretty as petals,
fluttering from the cherry tree.

The Emperor smiled at Li again.
Li smiled too, though by now
he was very hungry indeed.

"Friend Li," said the Emperor. "You gave us rice balls for our feast, you welcomed our singing and dancing. One thing more..."

"Just ask!" said Li.

"Now that our feast is over, will you sweep everywhere clean again?" asked the Emperor.

Li knew the mice were only little, so he was happy to help them tidy the palace. He hoped that sweeping would stop him feeling hungry.

The mice brought a brush and
a sack, and then scurried off,
squeaking with laughter.

When Li knelt to sweep away the crumbs, he saw piles of long-lost jewels and coins lying there.

"Take that rubbish away, Friend
Li," said the Emperor, smiling.
"Mice do not need such things!"

As Li swept the last coin into the
sack, he heard that song again:

"Roly-poly rice ball, roly-poly
rice ball, roly-poly rice ball,
roll right OUT!"

And Li was back under the
cherry tree, with his own
good fortune beside him.
He was never
hungry again.

Hopscotch has been specially designed to fit the requirements of the National Literacy Strategy. It offers real books by top authors and illustrators for children developing their reading skills.

There are 18 Hopscotch stories to choose from:

Marvin, the Blue Pig
Written by Karen Wallace, illustrated by Lisa Williams
0 7496 4619 5 (pbk)

Plip and Plop
Written by Penny Dolan, illustrated by Lisa Smith
0 7496 4620 9 (pbk)

The Queen's Dragon
Written by Anne Cassidy, illustrated by Gwyneth Williamson
0 7496 4618 7 (pbk)

Flora McQuack
Written by Penny Dolan, illustrated by Kay Widdowson
0 7496 4621 7 (pbk)

Willie the Whale
Written by Joy Oades, illustrated by Barbara Vagnozzi
0 7496 4623 3 (pbk)

Naughty Nancy
Written by Anne Cassidy, illustrated by Desideria Guicciardini
0 7496 4622 5 (pbk)

Run!
Written by Sue Ferraby, illustrated by Fabiano Fiorin
0 7496 4705 1 (pbk)

The Playground Snake
Written by Brian Moses, illustrated by David Mostyn
0 7496 4706 X (pbk)

"Sausages!"
Written by Anne Adeney, illustrated by Roger Fereday
0 7496 4707 8 (pbk)

The Truth about Hansel and Gretel
Written by Karina Law, illustrated by Elke Counsell
0 7496 4708 6 (pbk)

Pippin's Big Jump
Written by Hilary Robinson, illustrated by Sarah Warburton
0 7496 4710 8 (pbk)

Whose Birthday Is It?
Written by Sherryl Clark, illustrated by Jan Smith
0 7496 4709 4 (pbk)

The Princess and the Frog
Written by Margaret Nash, illustrated by Martin Remphry
0 7496 4891 0 (hbk)
0 7496 5129 6 (pbk)

Flynn Flies High
Written by Hilary Robinson, illustrated by Tim Archbold
0 7496 4889 9 (hbk)
0 7496 5130 X (pbk)

Clever Cat
Written by Karen Wallace, illustrated by Anni Axworthy
0 7496 4890 2 (hbk)
0 7496 5131 8 (pbk)

Moo!
Written by Penny Dolan, illustrated by Melanie Sharp
0 7496 4893 7 (hbk)
0 7496 5332 9 (pbk)

Izzie's Idea
Written by Jillian Powell, illustrated by Leonie Shearing
0 7496 5162 8 (hbk)
0 7496 5334 5 (pbk)

Roly-poly Rice Ball
Written by Penny Dolan, illustrated by Diana Mayo
0 7496 4894 5 (hbk)
0 7496 5333 7 (pbk)